Michael Peres and Patricia Cost

SnOwflAke
SCIENCE
Activity Book

"

Michael Peres and Patty Cost have a genuine talent to engage and delight the growing audience of readers who are curious about nature, art, discovery, and science. As a team, they engage and appeal to all age groups from children to adults who are delighted by the charming story of a snowflake.

Wendy Marks, Director of Finance and Administration Galleries,
University Gallery, Shop One, RIT

"

"

Students interested in Bentley's and Libbrecht's books on snowflakes, as well as budding meteorologists, will enjoy this book. It's something I can use to deepen interest in snowflake photography when I read Snowflake Bentley to our students in the library.

Vicky Polk, Library Media Specialist
Klem North Elementary School, Webster, NY

"

Schiffer Kids™

4880 Lower Valley Road, Atglen, PA 19310

Is It Snowing Yet?

Snowflakes are frozen water molecules that form into unique and
delicate crystals when the conditions are right. How does this happen?
A speck of dust high up in the sky attracts a water vapor molecule. Soon, more water
vapor and water droplets join the crystal. As it grows bigger, "wings" can develop on
the crystal. The activities in this book will teach you what all of this means.
Are you ready to learn about snowflakes?

To the Parent/Teacher/Assistant: Vocabulary words in blue are defined in the "Important Words" section at the back of the book, although the learner may figure out what they mean from their immediate contexts. Completing the activities in this book will help children understand and memorize these words. The Go Deeper sections throughout will give an older or more advanced child the chance to learn more.

WHAT YOU'LL NEED FOR THE MAIN ACTIVITIES IN THIS BOOK:

❄ Snowflake collector page

❄ White paper

❄ Colored pencils, crayons, or markers

❄ Large pieces of white paper

❄ Scissors

❄ Magnifying glass

❄ Thermometer

❄ A glass of water

❄ Ice cube

❄ Carpet or sweater and balloon

EACH ACTIVITY HAS AN OPPORTUNITY TO GO DEEPER

WHAT YOU'LL NEED FOR GOING DEEPER:

❄ Hygrometer

❄ A piece of black velvet

❄ Baking pan

❄ Eyedropper

❄ Small, empty picture frame, or glass slide

❄ Two colors of clay

❄ 12 toothpicks

❄ Several drinking straws

❄ Tablespoon

❄ Drinking glass

❄ Table salt

❄ Sewing needle taped to a pencil (adult supervision required)

❄ Smartphone

❄ Colored paper

LET'S KEEP A
Weather History Journal

You can start keeping a daily log of weather conditions to get ready for the first snowflakes of the year. Because these weather conditions can change many times during the day, record your weather information at the same time each day. For example, use your thermometer to read the temperature, and write this number on your chart next to "temperature." Use these meteorological terms for your measurements:

Temperature .... in degrees—use your thermometer

Sky appearance .... clear, partly sunny, broken clouds, cloudy

Precipitation .... showers, sleet, snow, blizzard, frost, fog, ice

Wind .... calm, breezy, windy, gusty

Humidity (if possible) .... the amount of water vapor that is present in the air

WEATHER HISTORY JOURNAL

	Date/Time	Sky Appearance	Temperature	Precipitation	Wind	Humidity
Day 1						
Day 2						
Day 3						
Day 4						
Day 5						
Day 6						
Day 7						

GO DEEPER

Thermometers show temperatures in degrees Fahrenheit or Celsius.
Which type of thermometer do you have? Some thermometers have both scales.
A hygrometer measures the amount of humidity in the air.
If your teacher has one, you can record humidity in your journal.

LET'S
Catch Snowflakes

Is it snowing outside?
In the winter, Michael and his snowflake hunter dogs look outside
every morning to see whether it's snowing.

You can use the snowflake collector pages in this book to catch snowflake crystals.
It will be easy to see the crystals on the paper because the white snow will
contrast with the black background.

The snowflake collector page has to be acclimated to the outside temperature
so that the snowflakes won't melt right away. This can take up to an hour.
Take your black paper outside to a garage or porch or put it out in a plastic bag
about one hour before you want to catch snowflakes.

Michael loves studying and
photographing snowflakes. He teaches
photomicrography, which is a big word
for "taking pictures through a
microscope."

GO DEEPER

Velvet is a type of fabric. Michael uses black velvet to catch snowflakes.
Why do you think it works better than paper?

The velvet must be **stable**, so Michael drapes it over a baking pan.
That way it won't flutter in the wind.

LET'S USE
a Magnifying Glass

A magnifying glass can enlarge small objects for looking at.
Take your magnifying glass with you when you go outside to catch snowflakes.
Then study them up close. Every time it snows, the snowflakes can look different.
The snowflakes on this page are from different storm systems.
Snowflakes can look very different even during the same storm.

GO DEEPER

You can make your own magnifying glass indoors. With adult supervision, take the back off a small picture frame so that you can see through the glass. Or use a glass slide. Put the object that you want to magnify on a flat surface. With an eyedropper, place one large drop of water on the glass. Hold the glass over the object and look through the drop of water. What do you see?

LET'S
Draw Snowflakes

It will be fun to draw your favorite snowflakes.
When you go outside, take along this book or a piece of white paper,
your snowflake collector pages or piece of black velvet, a pencil or crayon,
and your magnifying glass.
Catch snowflakes. Looking through the magnifying glass, draw your snowflakes.
But draw quickly! The crystals might start to melt or change.

MY SNOWFLAKES

GO DEEPER

There are many types of snowflake crystals. Can you identify the snowflake crystals that you caught?

Stellar plates

Needles

Dendritic snowflake

Granular snowflake

Granular snowflake

Capped columns

Columns

LET'S
Draw Hexagons

Some snowflakes have six wings (dendrites).
A six-sided shape is called a hexagon. These photos show the hexagon
in the middle of dendritic snowflakes.

DRAW A HEXAGON ON THIS PAGE.

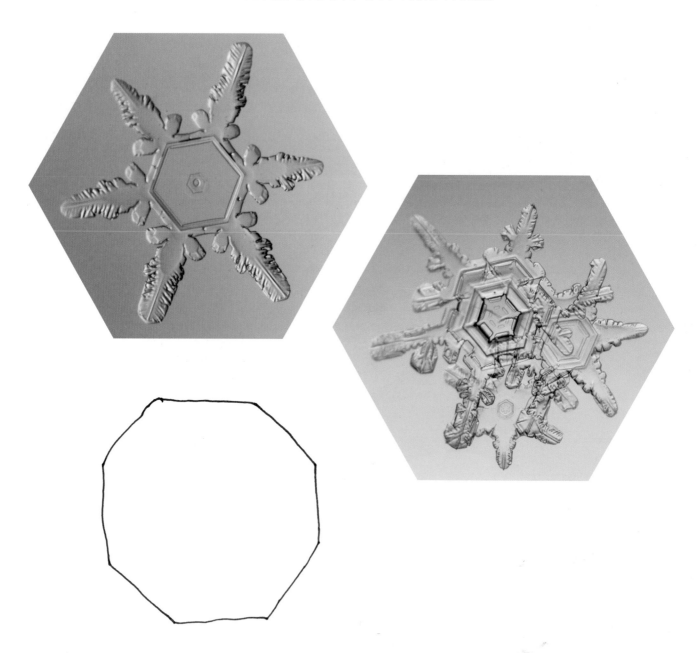

Now try drawing the following shapes: triangle, quadrilateral, square, pentagon, heptagon, octagon, circle, semicircle, oval, and blob!

WHY ARE NO
Two Snowflakes Alike?

When a piece of dust high up in the atmosphere attracts a molecule
of water vapor, the molecule jumps onto the piece of dust and bonds to it.
This attraction is called static electricity, the first variable of snowflake formation.
The amount of static electricity naturally present in the air changes all the time.

The tiny stellar plate now begins to move around in the sky. These embryonic snowflakes will have individual journeys. Along the way, weather conditions will affect the way they form:

Humidity How much water vapor is in the air

Temperature How cold it is

Wind How much the snowflake twirls and moves

Altitude of formation How high up the snowflake begins to form, and how long the snowflake stays aloft

Each of these conditions will change the way that the snowflake grows.
No wonder that no two snowflakes are the same!

GO DEEPER

THINK: What other groups of things have this quality—that no two are alike?

LET'S DRAW
A Water Molecule

A molecule is two or more atoms bonded together.
An atom is a building block for molecules. Think of it like this: If the word "snow" was a molecule, the letters *s*, *n*, *o*, and *w* would be the atoms. The letters bond or join together to make the word.

One oxygen atom and two hydrogen atoms join together to make one water molecule, like this.

We write it like this: H_2O.

DRAW A WATER MOLECULE HERE.

GO DEEPER

You can make a model of an ice crystal.

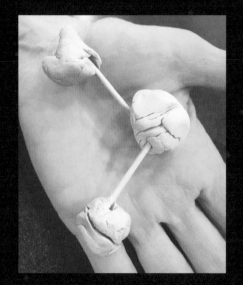

(1) Make a model of a water molecule: form two small balls of the same color of clay for the hydrogen atoms, and make one larger ball in a different color of clay for the oxygen atom. Use toothpicks to join the two clay hydrogen atoms to the clay oxygen atom. These toothpicks between the clay atoms in the clay molecule would be called molecular bonds.

(2) Make five more water molecule clay models.

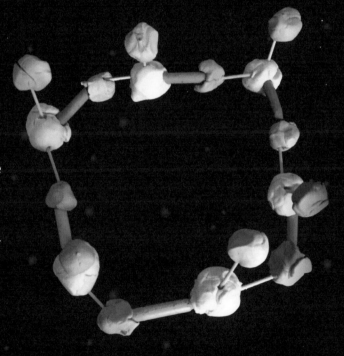

(3) Cut the drinking straws into thirds. Next, combine the six clay water molecules into a hexagon, using the straws, like this: Stick one piece of straw in one hydrogen ball from one water molecule, and stick the other end of the same straw into an oxygen ball from a different water molecule. Continue with all six water molecules, going around the hexagonal shape. These straw pieces between the clay molecules would be called hydrogen bonds. The leftover clay hydrogen balls from each clay water molecule can stick up in the air (looking for more molecules to join).

You might figure out that the hydrogen atoms sticking up in the air could become a part of another hexagonal ring of molecules, if more water vapor molecules join the crystal.

What other ways can you join the water molecules to make a hexagon?

LET'S FIND EXAMPLES OF THE
Three Phases of Water

(1) Can you pour it? Then it's in the **liquid phase**. Pour water into a clear glass.

(2) Do you breathe it in? Then it's in the **gaseous phase**, and it's called **water vapor**. You can see water vapor, also called steam, coming out of a pot of boiling water. Some of the boiling water **evaporates** into the air.

(3) Can you hold it with two fingers? Then it's **ice**, it's in the **solid phase**, and it's called a **crystal**. An ice cube is made up of many crystals.

A snowflake starts out as water vapor that freezes around a piece of dust. More water vapor is then attracted to it. All crystals start out small and then grow. When crystals are very small, they are not **visible**. As a crystal grows it becomes almost visible.

GO DEEPER

You can make crystals.

Pour two tablespoons of salt into half a glass of very hot water
and stir it until the salt dissolves.

Now put several drops of the dissolved salt solution onto
a glass picture frame and put a piece of black paper underneath it to add contrast.
It will grow salt crystals! Allow four hours.

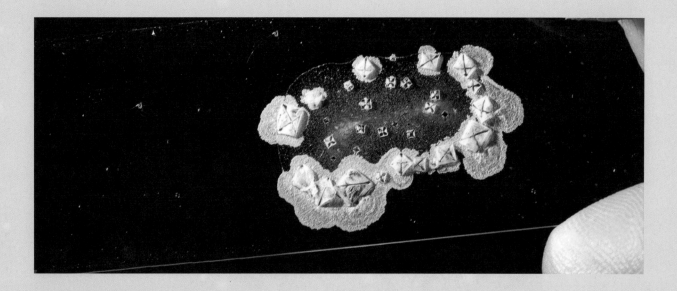

Look at the crystals with your magnifying glass. Are the salt crystals hexagons?

LET'S MAKE
Static Electricity

Blow up a balloon, tie it closed,
and then rub it back and forth on a carpet or sweater for a minute.
Now hold the balloon near a wall. What happens? If there's enough
humidity in the room, the balloon will stick to the wall.

The balloon sticks to the wall because of static electricity.
How does that work? When you rub the balloon on the carpet or a sweater,
some of the atoms from the balloon look for a new place to bond.
They try to bond to the wall.

In the same way, a water vapor molecule can be attracted
to a piece of dust high up in the cold atmosphere and bond to it,
if there is enough static electricity in the air.
More water vapor molecules may also be attracted to it.
The molecules then freeze into crystals if it's cold.

GO DEEPER

Michael uses static electricity to pick up his snowflakes.
With a sewing needle taped to a pencil, he points to the snowflake
on the piece of black velvet that he wants to photograph.
He moves the needle close to the snowflake, and it seems to jump
onto the needle because the molecules in the snowflake are attracted to the
molecules in the needle. Once the needle is holding the snowflake,
Michael moves it to a glass slide. With adult supervision,
you can try it outside too.

LET'S LOOK AT
Snowflake Photographs

Michael uses a special microscope camera in his garage to photograph snowflakes. Taking pictures of snowflakes is a challenging hobby. The air temperature is extremely important. If it's not cold enough outside (at least 25° Fahrenheit), it will be difficult to catch and look at the snowflakes. You can't plan ahead to photograph snowflakes.

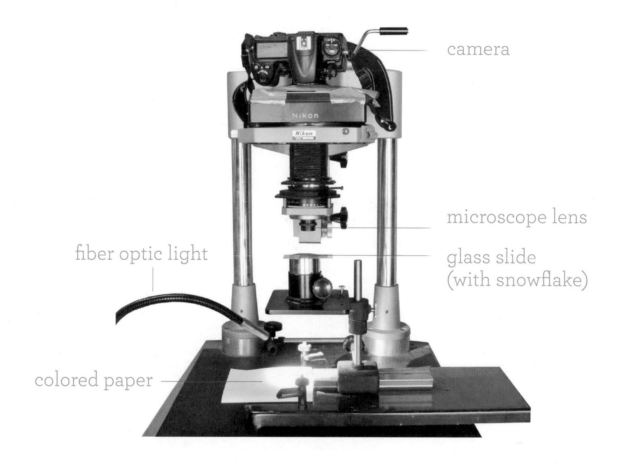

camera

microscope lens

fiber optic light

glass slide
(with snowflake)

colored paper

He says, "Being a snowflake photographer is almost like being a fireman. You have to be ready when the conditions are right. Each storm is a random event. You will not be in charge of the process. Instead, you have to be ready to go!

"Where I live, the temperature that produces the best crystals is between 15 and 25 degrees Fahrenheit.

"I keep my microscope outside so it will be cold when it snows. If the microscope stays inside and I bring a snowflake to it, the snowflake will melt immediately. It's OK for me to keep my camera inside, but all my other tools have to be outside in a garage or shed, waiting for action. I have to keep my snowflake-catching paper or velvet outside too."

GO DEEPER

You can photograph snowflakes with a smartphone.
If your phone's camera has an image size setting, set the 1x–2x setting to 2x.

The average smartphone will allow you to photograph a subject about
3 inches away. Try to move the snowflake to the glass picture frame with a piece
of colored paper underneath. Stay outside so the snowflake doesn't melt!
You can also buy a close-up lens adapter for a smartphone that will improve your
results. Or try photographing through your magnifying glass.

LET'S MAKE
Paper Snowflakes

DIRECTIONS:

❄ Cut a circle out of a big piece of white paper. It doesn't have to be perfect.

❄ Fold the circle in half to make a semicircle.

❄ This will be the hardest part: Fold the semicircle into thirds. It will become a wedge, like a piece of pie.

❄ Fold this wedge shape down the middle.

❄ Holding the bottom point of the wedge with the final fold on the left, make a cut in from the right side and then cut up to the top of the wedge (taking a chunk out of the right top corner of the wedge). Leave the left top of the wedge alone.

❄ Now cut out triangles and rectangles, keeping the left corner uncut. Cut with straight lines. Snowflakes are made up of ice crystals that have straight edges.

❄ Don't cut all the way through the paper from one side to the other, because that will destroy your snowflake!

❄ Carefully unfold your snowflake.

GO DEEPER

THINK: The snowflakes you cut out of paper will be symmetrical. Why aren't most natural snowflake crystals symmetrical?

LET'S REVIEW
Snowflake Facts

Water can exist as a solid (ice), a liquid (water), or a gas (water vapor).
Ice is made of many water crystals. All crystals start out small
and then grow. When crystals are very small, they are not visible.
As they grow, they eventually become visible.

All snowflakes start out as a grain of dust floating high up in the sky.
Water vapor is naturally attracted to the dust, and if it's very cold,
it freezes onto the dust in a structure called an ice crystal.
When more water vapor joins the ice crystal and freezes onto the
small structure, the crystal grows into a hexagonal (six-sided) plate.
The water vapor molecules form hexagonal patterns because
that's the way they fit best.

The hexagonal plate is the first stage of a snowflake crystal, and it has no wings. The crystal flies through the air, attracting more water vapor that freezes and locks onto it. As it grows, it can radiate outward, like a star, and then is called a stellar plate. Stellar plates have bumps or unbranched arms. As the crystal continues to grow, it can eventually become a stellar dendrite.

No two snowflakes are alike because of the individual paths
and experiences that the embryonic crystals experience before falling to Earth.
Each snowflake's size and shape is affected by:

❋ the altitude of its formation, or how far up in the atmosphere the plate first forms

❋ the temperature where the crystal forms and as it continues to grow

❋ the humidity in the air where the crystal forms and as it continues to grow

❋ the static electricity present in the atmosphere

❋ the time it takes until the crystal reaches Earth

THESE ARE THE OBSTACLES TO IDEAL SNOWFLAKE CRYSTAL FORMATION:

1mm

❋ If it's too cold (0–12° F), the snowflakes will be very small and thin.

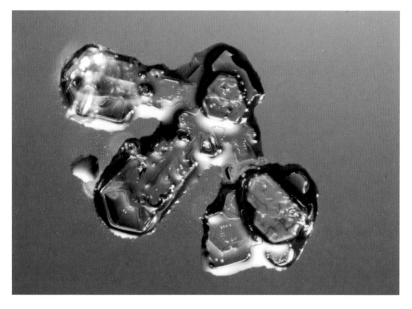

❄ If it's too warm (above 32° F), they'll begin to melt into water droplets immediately when captured.

❄ If the humidity is too high, the snowflakes will clump together.

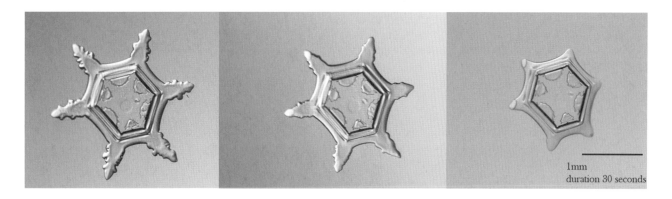

1mm
duration 30 seconds

❄ If the humidity is too low and the temperature is near freezing, the crystals can disappear or sublimate—that is, change into water vapor without melting.

LET'S TRY A
Crossword Puzzle

Across

1. an ice crystal that might grow into a snowflake

2. a measurement of the water vapor in the air

3. the solid phase of water

4. a type of fabric that has a thick, short pile on one side

5. exactly the same on both sides

6. air that surrounds the Earth

7. how high up in the atmosphere something is

8. the building blocks of molecules

Down

1. a shape that has six sides

2. the gaseous phase of water

3. how hot or cold something is

4. forms when a substance turns from a liquid phase to a solid phase, like ice or salt

5. one of the wings, or arms, of a snowflake

6. the smallest amount of a substance that has all the characteristics of that substance

7. able to be seen with the eyes

Snowflakes

LET'S DO A
Word Search

```
O X H D I U Q I L D H E T S
E C R Y S T A L S Y I T H Y
T L W S G E N A D I C L E B
A E R E I R G R E Q U I O R
M V M L D U O X Y G E N M S
I A D P K G A M C A M I A E
B P I C E A E T E S O F G K
U O U N A R W A L T L A N A
S R Q U T O A G S P E H I L
L A U R H U T T I O C R F F
R T T S E C E Q U I U E Y W
A E I C R T R I S R L N D O
P L W E D G A L M C E H I N
M A G N E W S W O T L E L S
E P R E C I P I T A T I O N
T S A R T N O C A W E T S T
```

Solid
Liquid
Gas
Ice
Water
Vapor

Evaporate
Temperature
Celsius
Fahrenheit
Hygrometer
Atom

Molecule
Crystal
Snowflake
Wedge
Hydrogen
Oxygen

Precipitation
Magnify
Contrast

LET'S MATCH IMPORTANT
Words and Their Meanings

WRITE THE LETTER OF THE CORRECT ANSWER ON THE LINE NEXT TO THE IMPORTANT WORD.

A. "wing" or arm of a snowflake

B. the measurement of the water vapor in the air

C. resistant to a change of position

D. all the air that surrounds the Earth

E. a shape that has six sides

F. the gaseous phase of water

G. a device used to measure temperature

H. to go from a liquid phase to a gaseous phase

I. to go from a solid phase to a liquid phase

J. the solid phase of water

K. the falling of water, in any form, to Earth

L. a measurement of how cold or hot it is

M. able to be seen with the human eye

N. the first stage of a snowflake crystal

O. electricity that has gathered in one place

P. to become accustomed to new conditions

___ Ice

___ Precipitation

___ Temperature

___ Hexagonal plate

___ Static electricity

___ Dendrite

___ Visible

___ Thermometer

___ Stable

___ Hexagon

___ Atmosphere

___ Acclimate

___ Melt

___ Humidity

___ Water vapor

___ Evaporate

LET'S
Color Snowflakes

Michael sometimes adds colors to his snowflake photographs. To add color, he shines a special light on a piece of colored paper below the glass slide that holds the snowflake. The paper colors the light that is **reflected** up through the snowflake and microscope lens, all the way up to the camera.

You can color these snowflake pictures by using one color or a rainbow of colors.

GO DEEPER

THINK: Michael usually uses blue to color his snowflakes.
Do you know why?

Michael uses blue because blue represents cool or cold temperatures.

ADDITIONAL RESOURCES
Snowflake Books

Bentley, W. A. *Snowflakes in Photographs*. Mineola, NY: Dover, 2000.

Cassino, Mark. *The Story of Snow*. San Francisco: Chronicle Books, 2009.

Cost, Patricia, and Michael Peres. *Michael Photographs a Snowflake*. Rochester, NY: Fossil, 2016.

Gibbons, Gail. *It's Snowing!* New York: Holiday House, 2011.

Halpern, Julie. *Toby and the Snowflakes*. Boston: Houghton Mifflin, 2004.

Harper, Lizzie. *Art for Mindfulness: Winter Wonderland*. London: Harper Collins, 2015.

Keats, Ezra Jack. *The Snowy Day*. New York: Viking, 1962.

Libbrecht, Kenneth. *The Art of the Snowflake: A Photographic Album*. St. Paul, MN: Voyageur, 2007.

Libbrecht, Kenneth. *The Little Book of Snowflakes*. St. Paul, MN: Voyageur, 2004.

Libbrecht, Kenneth. *The Secret Life of a Snowflake: An Up-Close Look at the Art & Science of Snowflakes*. Minneapolis: Voyageur, 2009.

Libbrecht, Kenneth. *Snowflakes*. Minneapolis: Voyageur, 2008.

Martin, Jacqueline Briggs. *Snowflake Bentley*. Boston: Sandpiper, 1998.

Poydar, Nancy. *Snip, Snip . . . Snow!* New York: Holiday House, 1997.

Shulevitz, Uri. *Snow*. New York: Farrar Straus Giroux, 1998.

Williams, Judith. *How Come It's Snowing?* Berkeley Heights, NY: Enslow, 2015.

Winters, Angela. *How to Make a Paper Snowflake*. Katonah, NY: Kim Pathways, 1990.

IMPORTANT WORDS

acclimate: To become accustomed to new conditions, like temperature

altitude of formation: How high up in the atmosphere a snowflake is initially formed

atmosphere: All the air that surrounds the Earth

atom: The basic building block for molecules and for all matter in the universe

bonded: Chemically joined together, like bonds in a water molecule, H_2O

Celsius: A temperature scale that registers the freezing point at 0 degrees and the boiling point at 100 degrees

contrast: To make things more visible

crystal: A small amount of a substance that has many sides and is formed when the substance turns into a solid, like a snowflake, or salt

dendrite: A "wing" or arm of a snowflake

embryonic: Being in a very early stage of development

enlarge: To cause something to appear larger than it really is

evaporate: To go from a liquid phase to a gaseous phase; water evaporates

Fahrenheit: A temperature scale that registers the freezing point at 32 degrees and the boiling point at 212 degrees

gaseous phase: One of the three phases of matter in which the molecules and atoms are free to spread out and thus aren't easily seen

glass slide: A thin, flat, rectangular piece of glass that is used for microscopic specimen observation

hexagon: A shape that has six sides

hexagonal plate: The first stage of a snowflake crystal, with no wings

humidity: The measurement of the amount of water vapor in the air

hydrogen: The simplest possible atom. It is the first element in the periodic table.

hydrogen bond: A partly electrostatic attraction between one hydrogen atom that is already bound to another atom in a molecule, and another hydrogen atom

hygrometer: A small instrument that measures humidity

ice: The solid phase of water

ice crystal: Another term for the solid phase of water

liquid phase: The state of matter in which a substance shows a readiness to flow, has little or no tendency to disperse, and is incapable of being compressed

magnify: To make something appear larger or more important than it really is

magnifying glass: A small, usually plastic lens that makes an object appear larger to the human eye than it really is

melt: To go from a solid phase to a liquid phase, as in ice melting

meteorological: Pertaining to the science that deals with what happens in the atmosphere, especially weather and weather conditions

microscope camera: A special microscope that has a camera attached at the top

molecular bond: When atoms join together to form a molecule, they can be said to have a molecular bond.

molecule: The smallest amount of a substance that has all the characteristics of that substance

oxygen: A very common element. It is one of the main elements that make up air, and it is essential for the survival of plants and animals.

photomicrography: taking pictures through a microscope

precipitation: The falling of water, in any form, from the sky to the Earth. It can be rain, hail, sleet, snow, frost, fog, or dew.

reflect: To return from a surface, such as light reflecting from a mirror

solid phase: A state of matter characterized by particles arranged such that their shape and volume are relatively stable

stable: Resistant to a change of position, not easily moved or disturbed

static electricity: Electricity that has gathered in one place. For example, static electricity on a balloon can make it stick to a wall or your clothing. The word "static" means something that does not move.

stellar plate: The second phase of some snowflake crystal development. As it grows, it begins to radiate out like a star.

sublimate: To change from a solid to a gas, or a gas to a solid, skipping over the liquid phase, like a snowflake evaporating (changing into water vapor) without melting

symmetrical: Exhibiting exactly the same characteristics on opposite sides

temperature: A measurement of how cold or hot something is

thermometer: A device used to measure temperature

velvet: A type of fabric that has a thick, short pile on one side

visible: Able to be seen with the human eye

water vapor: The gaseous phase of water

weather: The state of the atmosphere at a given time and place, with respect to variables such as temperature, humidity, and wind

wedge: Something in a triangular shape, like a piece of pie

ANSWER KEYS

Crossword

Important Words and Their Meanings

J__ Ice

K__ Precipitation

L__ Temperature

N__ Hexagonal plate

O__ Static electricity

A__ Dendrite

M__ Visible

G__ Thermometer

C__ Stable

E__ Hexagon

D__ Atmosphere

P__ Acclimate

I__ Melt

B__ Humidity

F__ Water vapor

H__ Evaporate

Word Search

ABOUT THE AUTHORS

Michael Peres is a professor of biomedical photography at Rochester Institute of Technology in Rochester, New York. He teaches photomicrography and other applications of photography in science and has been actively publishing for most of his career. He has won many prestigious awards. Michael's snowflake photographs have been featured on CNN and the Weather Channel, in *Time* magazine, and in numerous books.

Patricia Cost is an editor, writer, and designer. She wrote *The Bentons: How an American Father and Son Changed the Printing Industry*, and collaborated with Michael Peres on a picture book, *Michael Photographs a Snowflake*.

Artist Lizzie Harper drew the snowflakes to color, based on Michael's photographs. She is a natural-history illustrator who works in watercolor, pencil, pen and ink, colored pencil, and acrylics. Lizzie studied zoology and illustration and works from her garden studio at her home in Hay-On-Wye, England. She also drew many of Michael's other snowflake photographs for a coloring book that she coauthored with Christina Hart-Davies, titled *Art for Mindfulness: Winter Wonderland*.